Digger and Daisy

Go to the Doctor

PAWS FOR YOUR FLU SHOT!

By Judy Young

Illustrated by Dana Sullivan

Text Copyright © 2014 Judy Young
Illustration Copyright © 2014 Dana Sullivan

Sleeping Bear Press™

315 E. Eisenhower Parkway, Ste. 200
Ann Arbor, MI 48108
www.sleepingbearpress.com

Printed and bound in the United States.

10 9 8 7 6 5 4 3 2 1 (case)
10 9 8 7 6 5 4 3 2 1 (pbk)

Library of Congress Cataloging-in-Publication Data

Young, Judy.
Digger and Daisy go to the doctor / written by Judy Young ; illustrated
by Dana Sullivan.
pages cm
Summary: Digger is not feeling well but after his sister, Daisy, convinces him to go see a doctor
she must still persuade him to be brave by getting her own examination.
ISBN 978-1-58536-845-7 (hard cover) — ISBN 978-1-58536-846-4 (paper back)
[1. Sick—Fiction. 2. Physicians—Fiction. 3. Dogs—Fiction. 4. Brothers
and sisters—Fiction.] I. Sullivan, Dana, illustrator. II. Title.
PZ7.Y8664Dif 2014
[E]—dc23
2013050680

For Katelyn and Madison Mace
—Judy

To my sister, Caitlin, who likes to go first.
—Dana

The sun is up.

Daisy gets out of bed.

Digger does not.

"Get up, Digger," says Daisy.

"I do not want to," Digger says.

"I do not feel good."

Daisy looks at Digger.

He does not look good.

"You must go to the doctor,"

Daisy says.

"I do not want to go," says Digger.

"I will get a shot."

"A shot will make you feel better,"

Daisy says.

"No, it will hurt," Digger says.

"You must be brave, Digger.

It will only hurt a little," Daisy

says. "Then you will feel better."

Digger and Daisy go to the doctor.
"Jump up here," the doctor says
to Digger.

"No," Digger says.

"You will give me a shot."

"You must be brave, Digger,"
Daisy says. "Look at me."
Daisy jumps up.

Then Digger jumps up, too.

"Let me look in your eyes,"
the doctor says.

"No," says Digger.

"You must be brave, Digger,"

says Daisy.

"Look. Look at me."

Daisy opens her eyes wide.

The doctor looks in her eyes.

"See, Digger. It does not hurt,"

Daisy says.

"Okay," says Digger.

"Let me look in your ears,"
says the doctor.
"No," says Digger.

"You must be brave, Digger,"
says Daisy.

"Look. Look at me."

The doctor looks in her ears.
"See, Digger. It does not hurt,"
Daisy says.

"Okay," says Digger.

"Now let me see in your mouth,"
the doctor says.

"No," says Digger.

"You must be brave, Digger,"
says Daisy. "Look. Look at me."
Daisy opens her mouth wide.

The doctor looks in her mouth.
"See, Digger. It does not hurt,"
says Daisy.

"Okay," says Digger.

"That is all," says the doctor.

"I am done now."

"Do I have to get a shot?"

says Digger.

"No," says the doctor.

"You have a cold. That is all.

You will feel better soon."

"See, Digger," says Daisy.

"That did not hurt."

"Can we go now?" says Digger.

"No," says the doctor.

"Digger does not need a shot.

But you do, Daisy.

Turn around, Daisy."

Daisy does not turn around.

"I do not want a shot," she says.

"It will hurt."

"You must be brave, Daisy,"
says Digger.

"You said it will only hurt a little."

Look for other books in the Digger and Daisy series

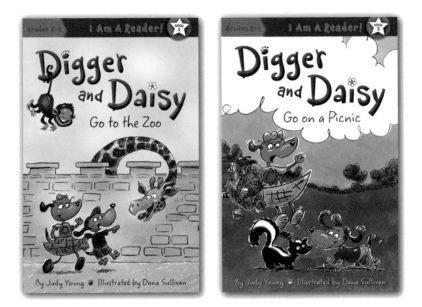

Digger and Daisy Go to the Zoo

"In this early reader, a dog learns from his sister what he can and cannot do like other animals on a visit to the zoo. . . . It's a lovely little tribute to sibling camaraderie . . . . this work is a welcoming invitation to read and a sweet encouragement to spend time with siblings."

—*Kirkus Reviews*